Mohandas Karamchand
(Mo-hun-dhaas Ka-rum-ch-un-dh)
Gandhi

(such a long name!)

wanted

everyone

to be treated the

same,

No matter how they **looked**

or the **colour** of their skin,

Or the way they **spoke** or their place of **origin.**

Place of Origin:
The place where a person was born or the place they grew up in.

Born in
Porbandar
(Po-r-bun-dh-u-r)

a small Indian town,

He grew up to become a person of

great renown.

Renown: Fame

He was a shy and playful little boy

Who loved reading stories and playing with his toys.

Later, he went to London

to study law,

Law: Rules which everyone in a country has to follow

And fought every **injustice** that he saw.

Injustice: When something is not fair

When he was in

Satyagraha House, Joburg

South Africa, he

Worked hard for
racial equality,

Racial Equality: Treating everyone the same no matter how different they look

He even helped India win
Independence

Independence: Freedom from being ruled by someone another country.
(India had been ruled by the British for around 200 years until August 15th, 1947.)

With the help of
non violent resistance,

Non Violent Resistance: Protesting (saying no) in a peaceful way (without fighting)

Which means if you do not like what someone says,

There are many
kind and **peaceful** ways

Of saying **no**
and making them see

Your **point of view**
and why you disagree.

Point of view: What you or someone else think about something

Mahatma Gandhi was courageous,

and a good leader too,

Courageous: Brave

A wonderful person — just like you!

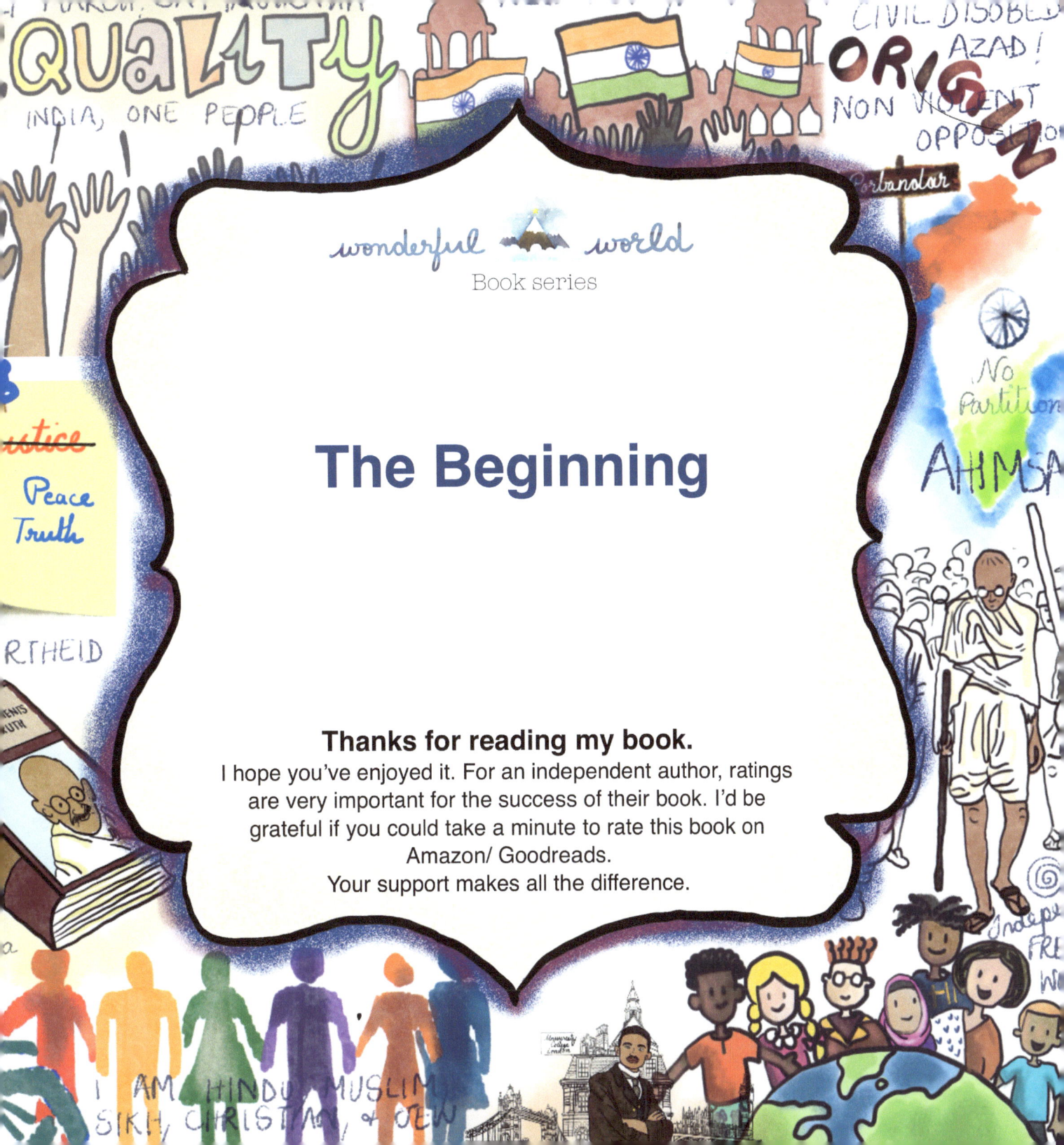

Glossary

Renown: Fame

Injustice: When something is not fair

Law: Rules which everyone in a country has to follow

Racial Equality: Treating everyone the same no matter how different they look

Non Violent Resistance: Protesting (saying no) in a peaceful way (without fighting)

Independence: Freedom from being ruled by someone another country. (India had been ruled by the British for around 200 years until August 15th, 1947.)

Point of view: What you or someone else think about something

Courageous: Brave

GANDHI

Timeline

2nd October 1869
Mohandas Gandhi is born in Porbandar (seaside town in Gujarat, India) to Karamchand and Putlibai Gandhi.

1882
13-year-old Mohandas was married to 14-year-old Kasturbai Gokuldas Kapadia (affectionately to "Ba") in an arranged marriage – which was normal in those times.

1888
Gandhi's first child, Harilal, was born. Gandhi travelled to London to study law at University College London.

1893
Gandhi went to South Africa to work as a lawyer. This experience marked a turning point in his life as he began to confront racial discrimination and injustice.

1919
Gandhi launched the non-cooperation movement against British rule in India, advocating for peaceful resistance and nonviolent protests.

1915
Gandhi returned to India from South Africa and started advocating for India's independence from British rule. He often fasted, and was often imprisoned during this struggle.

1906
Gandhi initiated nonviolent resistance, which he termed 'Satyagraha' (force of truth) during protests against the unfair laws in South Africa.

1930
Gandhi led the Salt March, a significant act of civil disobedience against British salt taxes, sparking widespread civil unrest across India.

1942
Gandhi launched the Quit India Movement, demanding an end to the British ruling India.

15th August 1947
India gained independence from British rule. However, the country was split into India and Pakistan, leading to a lot of fighting.

30th January 1948
Gandhi was killed in Delhi, India, on his way to the multi-faith prayers he held every evening.

Charkha
(Ch-ur-kh-aa)

The charkha was the spinning wheel used by Gandhi to weave khadi (kh-aa-dh-ee) cloth which he wore.

Sabarmati Ashram
A self-sufficient community Gandhi created

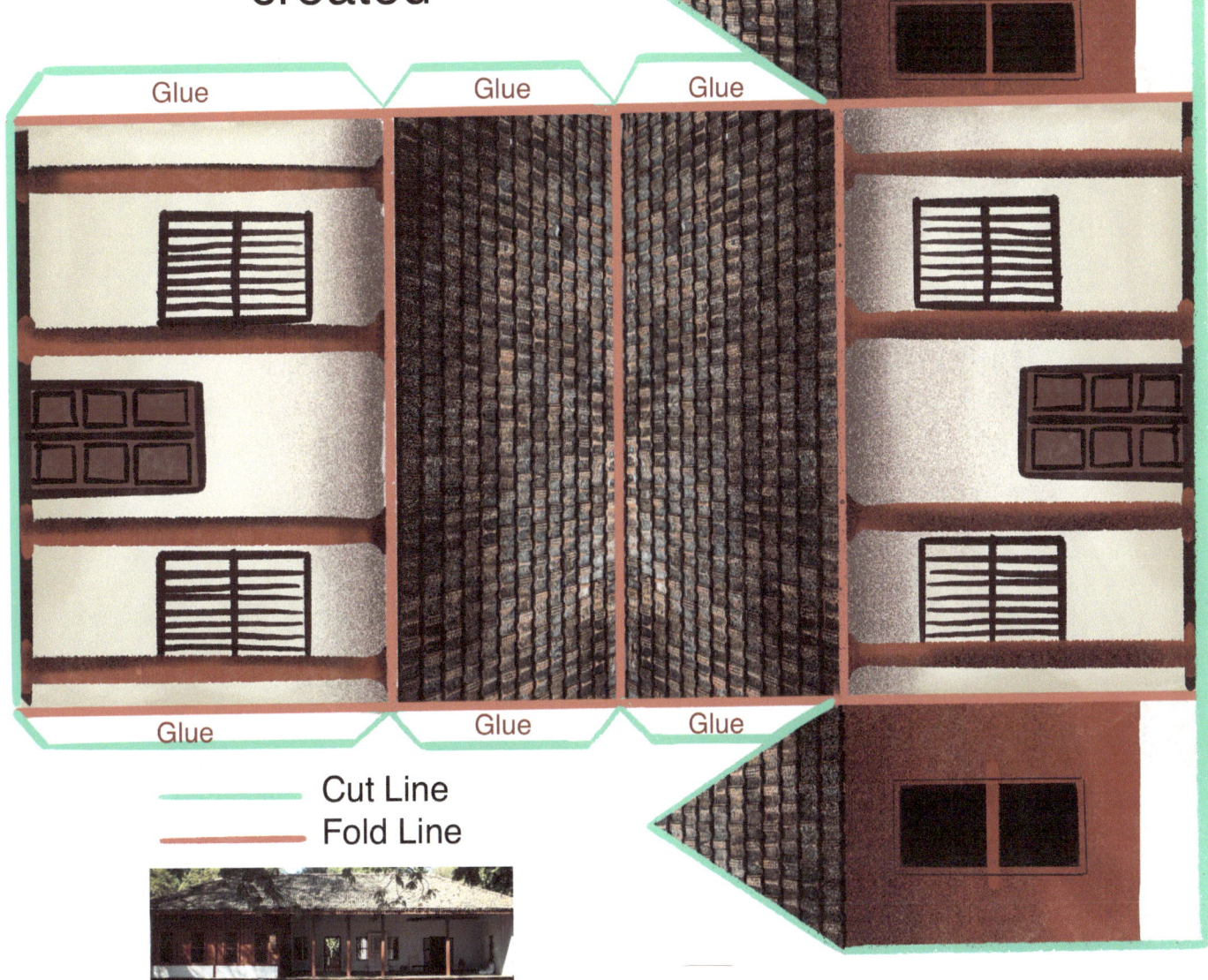

HELLO

Thank you for reading my book!

As an Indian, 'Gandhi' was a name I'd grown up hearing. Comic books, storybooks, history lessons - there was a lot of material about this unusual man, not to mention the thick biography by Louis Fischer featuring a picture of Ben Kingsley (!) from the movie 'Gandhi' on the cover.

Despite all this, researching about Gandhi for this picture book was fascinating! It's hard to imagine a world leader as a shy young man who stammered. But that was the truth.

Gandhi *was* a shy young man with a long, unusual name. Apparently, he was so nervous during his first court case that he fled the courtroom! However, he grew to become one of the most eloquent leaders of the world, in India and in South Africa. At a time when India was fighting for Independence leading to unimaginable acts of violence, this simply dressed, khadhi-clad, mild-mannered man shocked everyone by suggesting 'non-violence' and 'civil disobedience' as the best means of protest.

If humanity produces people such as this, there is hope for us, don't you agree?

Ramya

FREE

Check out
www.ramyajulian.com/picturebooks

www.ramyajulian.com

Also in this series

NEXT IN LINE: MANY MANY MORE WONDERFUL DIVERSE HEROES

TO MY NEWSLETTER
For the latest news and free printables
www.ramyajulian.com

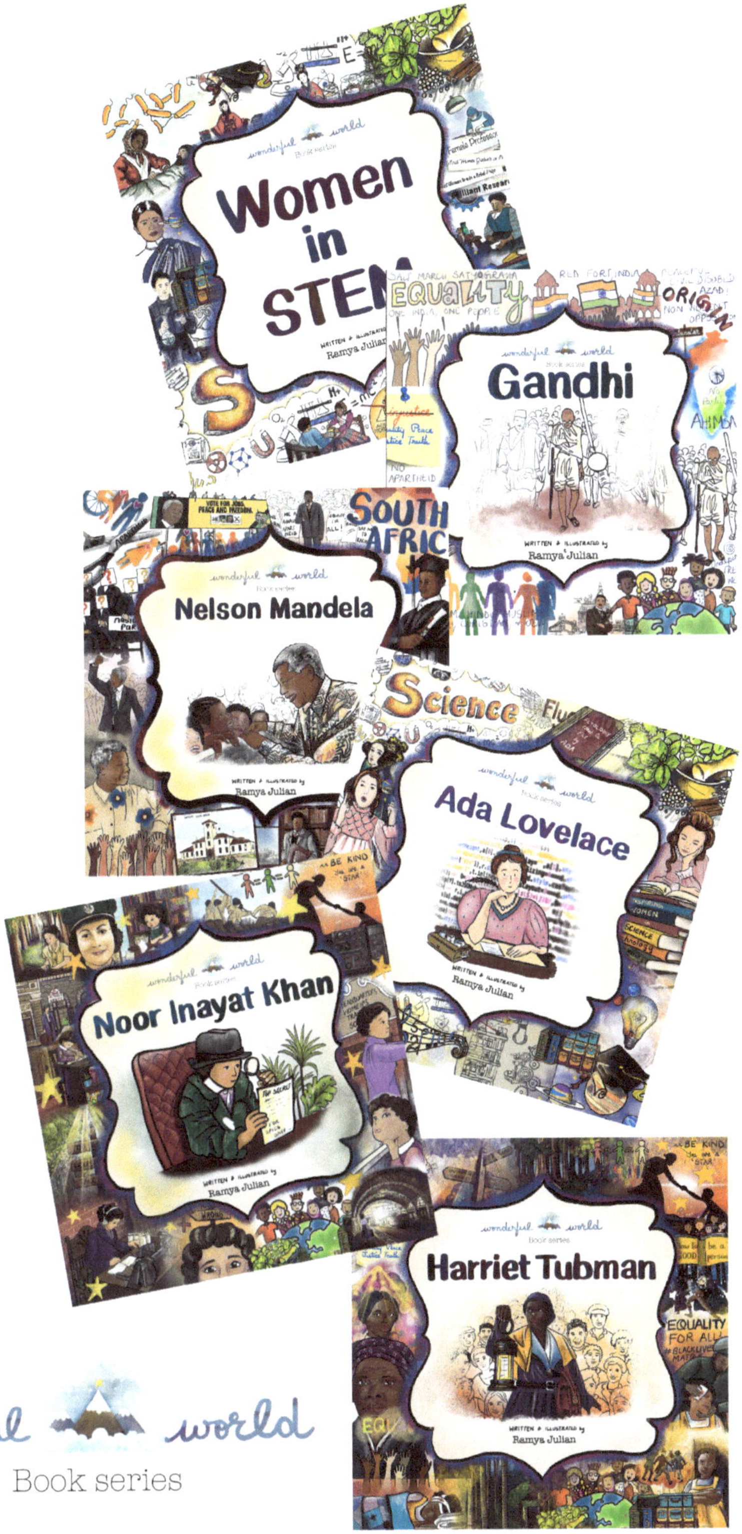

@RAMYAJULIAN

wonderful world
Book series